For every child facing a challenge
and for Benjamin, about whom this book was inspired,
Sam, Marc, Mum and Sir Kaye with love and thanks – J.B.

To everyone who sings in a choir, small or big.
Because the sound of your voice with all the others creates
the magic of harmony and makes our hearts happy – F.G.

EGMONT

We bring stories to life

First published in Great Britain 2019 by Egmont UK Limited,
The Yellow Building, 1 Nicholas Road, London W11 4AN

www.egmont.co.uk

Text copyright © Julie Ballard 2019
Illustrations copyright © Francesca Gambatesa 2019

The moral rights of the author and illustrator have been asserted.

ISBN 978 1 4052 8796 8

THE DINOSAUR
WHO LOST HER VOICE

JULIE BALLARD & FRANCESCA GAMBATESA

EGMONT

In wild and prehistoric woods
A long-lost time ago,

One dinosaur sang sweetly and
Her name was Milly Jo.

Her songs weaved spells of happiness,
By day and starry night.

Her friends would beam and sway in time,
They'd dance, not stomp and fight.

"Your singing's truly **magical**,"
They sighed. "Oh, what a tone!
Your voice is such a precious gift.
The **best** we've ever known."

But one hot and steamy summer's night
A storm raged all around.
Great forks of lightning crackled
And the rain began to pound.

"Quick! Run for cover!" Milly cried.
But then a tree went **CRASH!**
Poor Milly didn't stand a chance.
It struck her neck –

KER–BASH!

Next morning, all the dinosaurs
Begged Milly for a song.
But not a **single** note
came out.

They roared,
"There's something wrong!"

Her voice was damaged by the tree!
She couldn't say a word.
She tried her best to sing a note
But **nothing** could be heard.

Her friends howled:
"This is just so sad!"

Then Stegosaurus said:
"Her singing brought us so much joy. Let's sing to her instead!"

They did their best
to sing a song:

"A-SQUEAKY-
SQUAWK!
SHRIEK-BOOM!"

It wasn't good – and Milly knew
Her friends were out of tune.

As Milly listened to their din
She knew she must be **strong**.
She tapped a baton, mimed some words
And taught her friends a **song**.

She showed them all her music books
She pointed out the trills,

The highs, the lows,
the louds and softs
And other singing skills.

With gestures, smiles and tapping feet
She trained them **all** to be . . .

A troupe of tuneful dinosaurs
Who sang in harmony.

The band of friends
kept practising,
And soon they
sounded **great**.

"It's time to stage a show!" they cried.
"Hurray! Let's set a date!"

The **big day** came, and Milly soothed
Their nerves before the show.
She led one final practice, then . . .
The wind began to **blow**!

And as the choir prepared to sing
The rain began to pour.
The audience grew fidgety
And some began to . . .

ROAR!

With jitters, Milly led her choir –
They put on quite a show!

Their symphonies were wonderful.
The crowd all cheered, "Bravo!"

The friends all sang so perfectly
To lull the dinosaurs.
They calmed those wild, unruly hearts
And stilled their frightful roars.

As Milly dazzled brightly
In her choir's first ever show,
The sun peeped through the stormy clouds
And set the stage aglow.

The sky turned blue,
the rays beamed down
And bathed the choir in light.

And, in that instant, Milly knew

That things would be all right.

For, **best of all**, she'd shown the world
That special summer's day,
That she could do **amazing** things –
Just in a different way.

The dinosaurs clapped loudly and
They cheered "Encore!" and "Wow!"
Then Milly and her choir stepped forward
And took a well-earned bow!